I Did It!

I Did It!

Michael Emberley

I Like to Read® COMICS

HOLIDAY HOUSE · NEW YORK

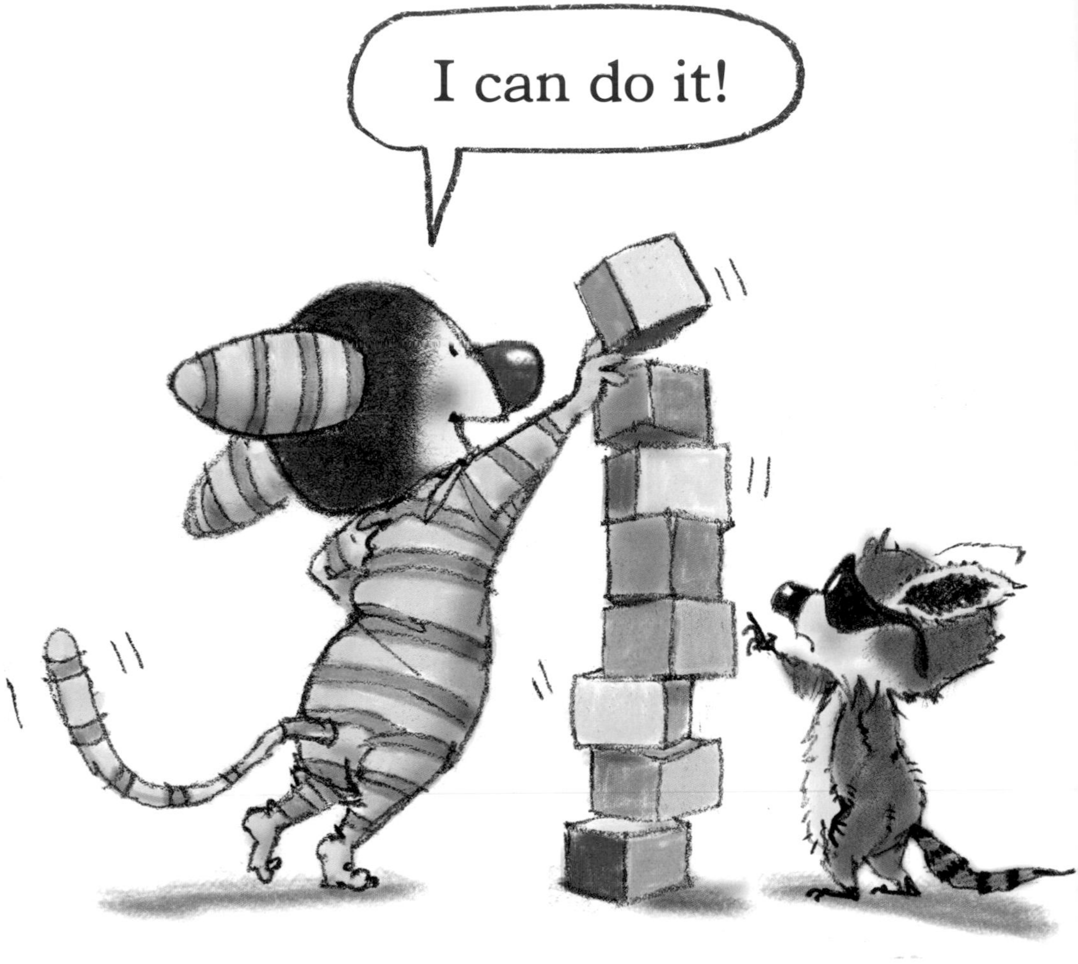
I can do it!

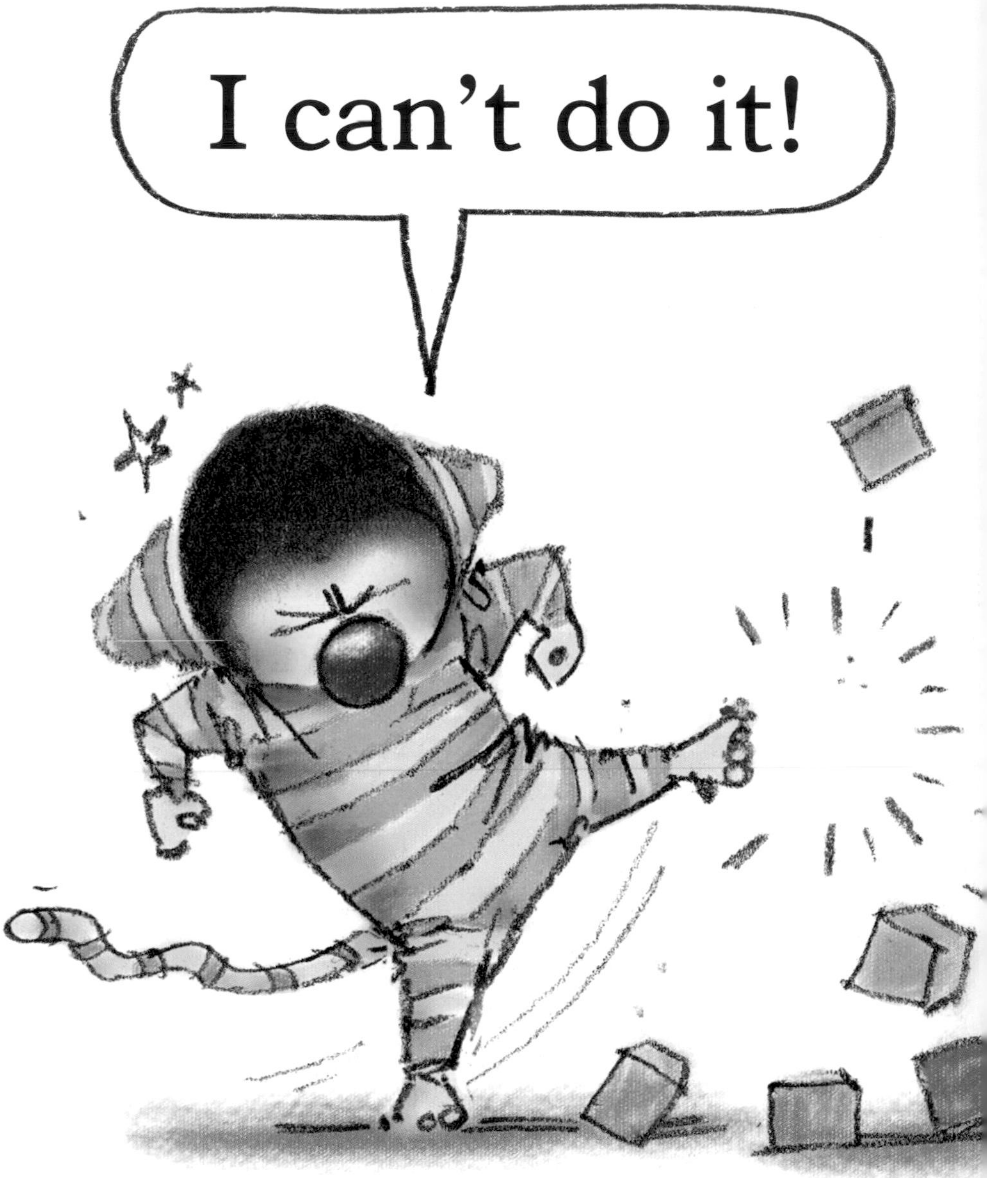
I can't do it!

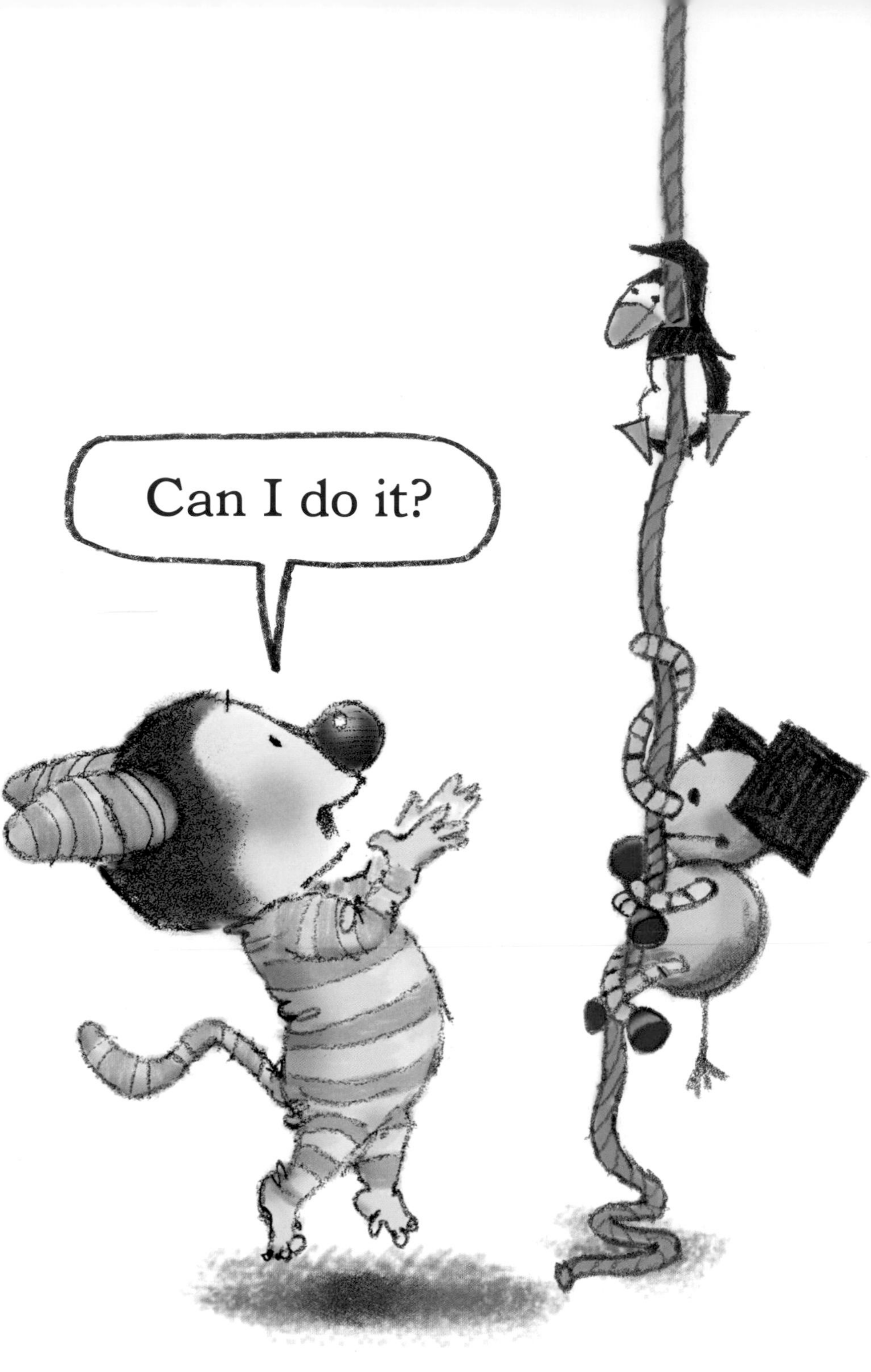
Can I do it?

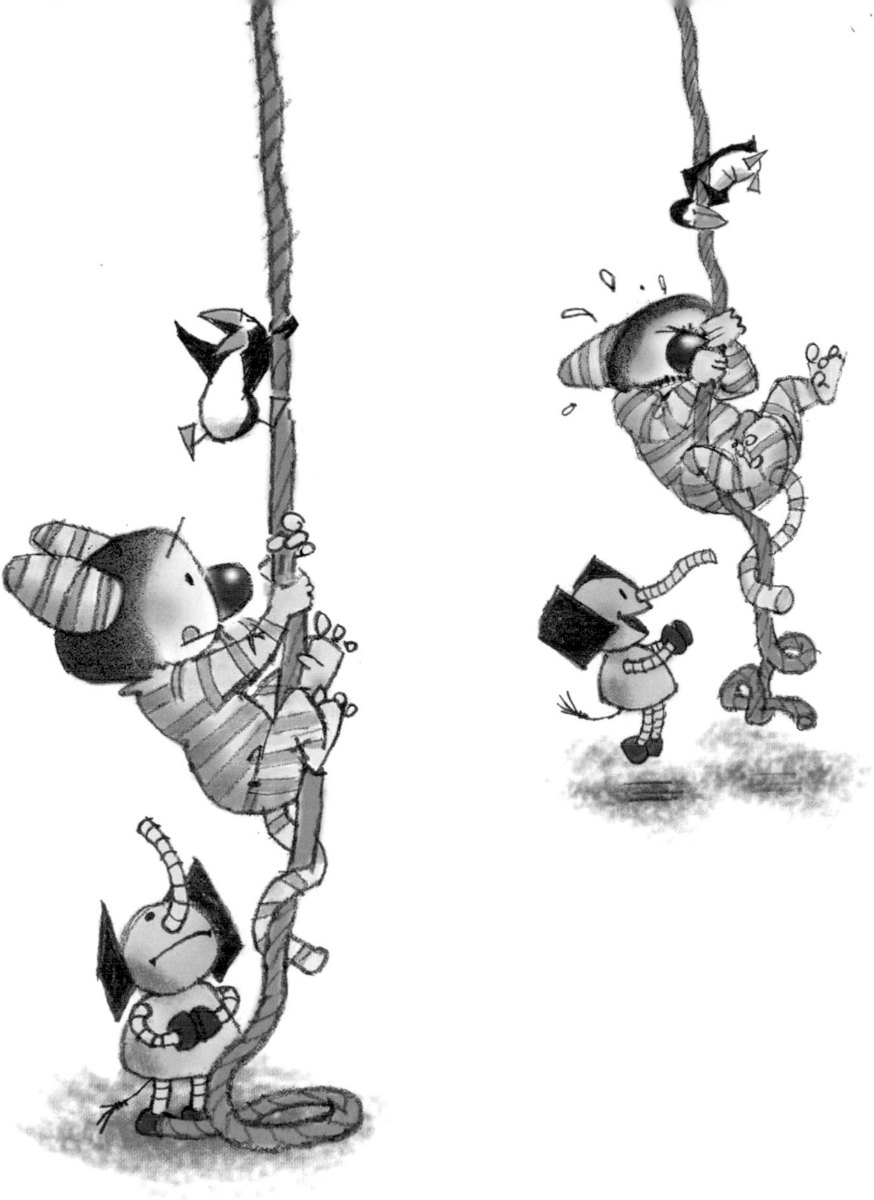

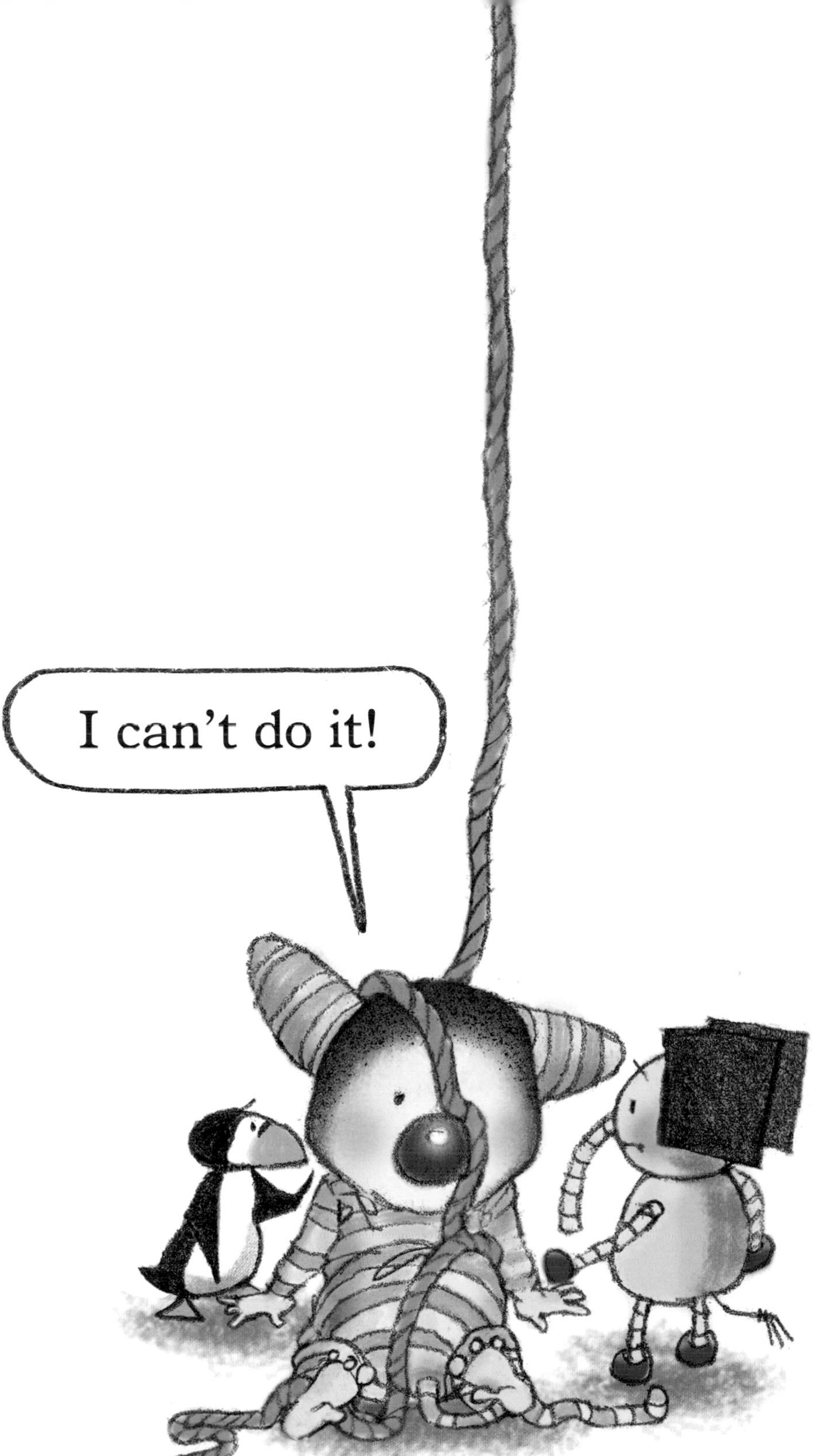
I can't do it!

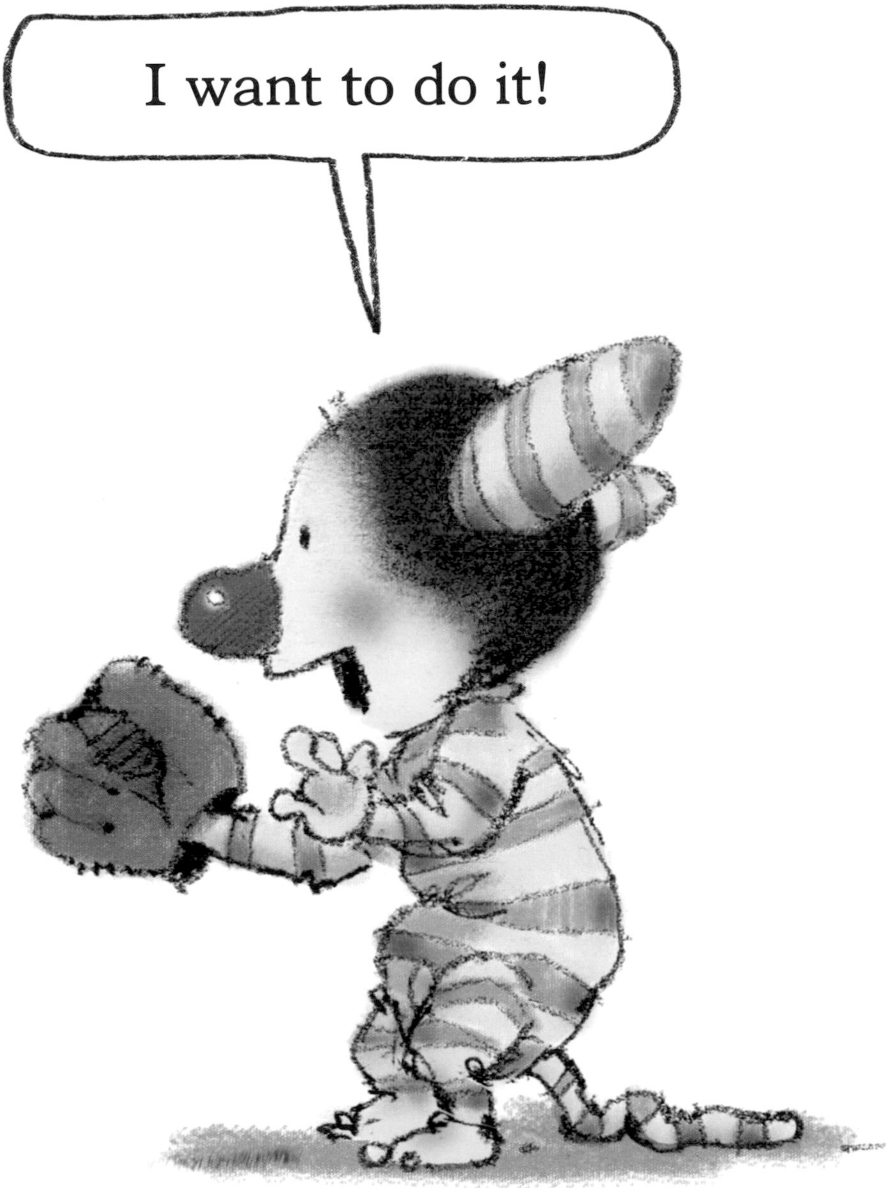
I want to do it!

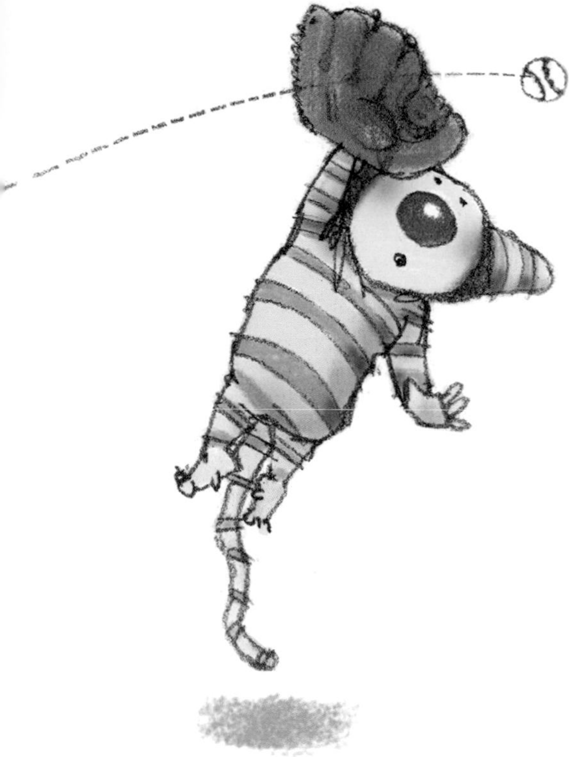

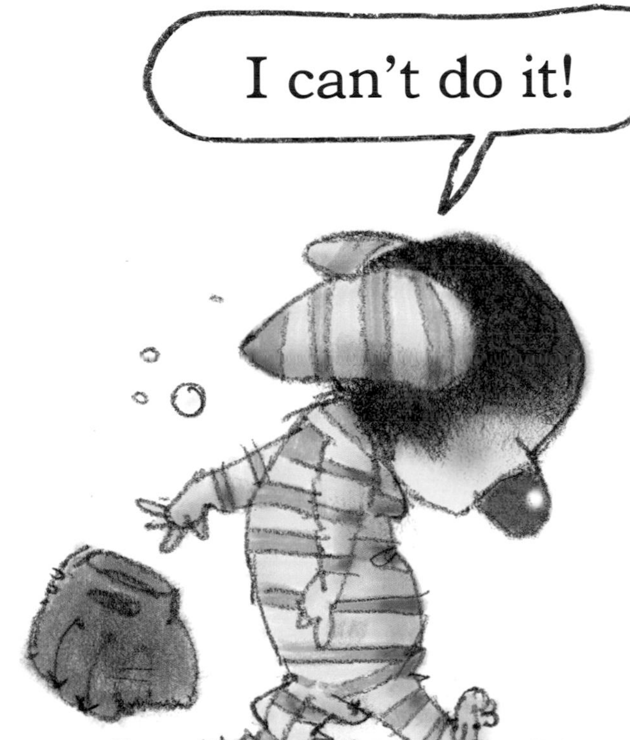
I can’t do it!

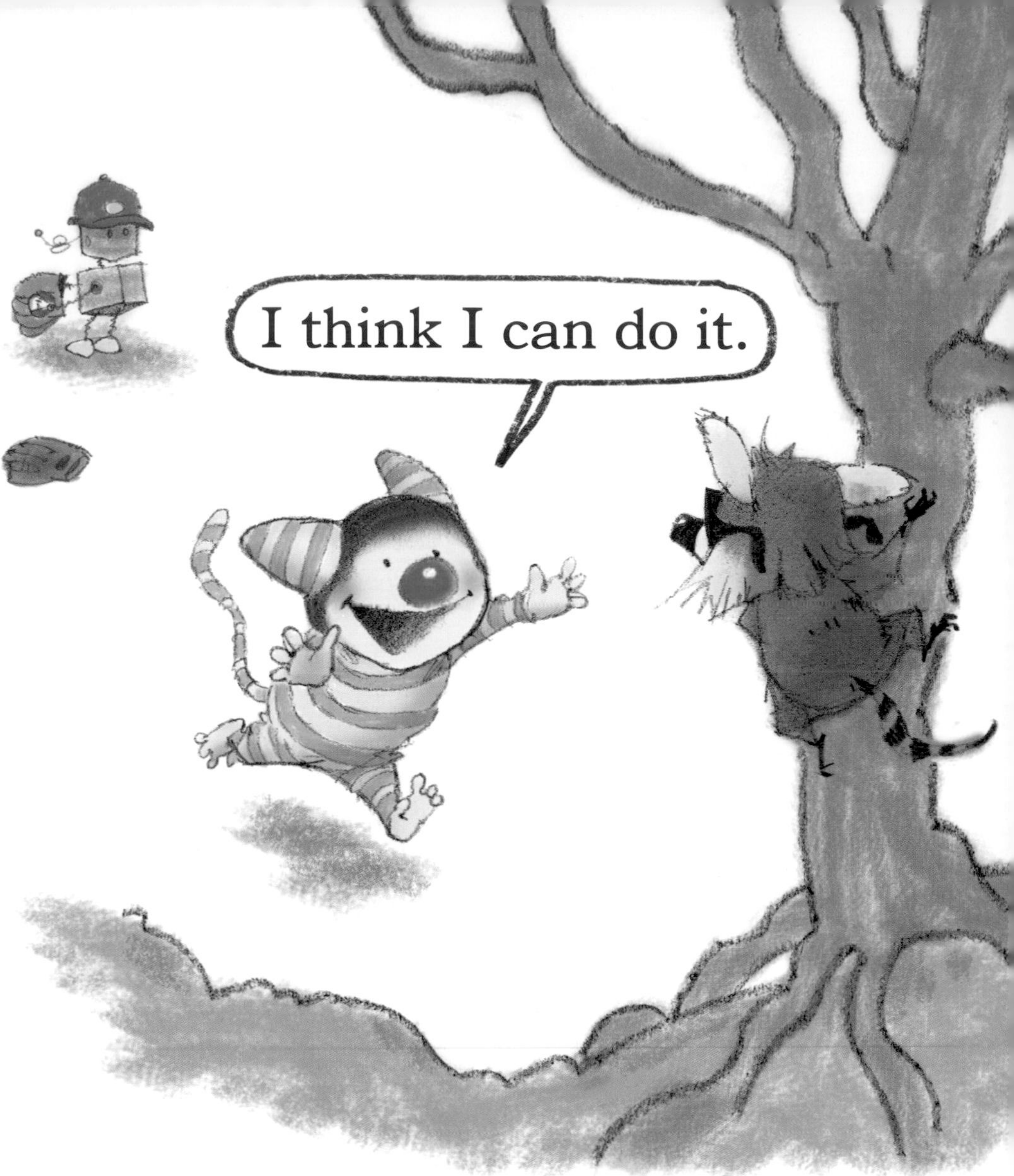
I think I can do it.

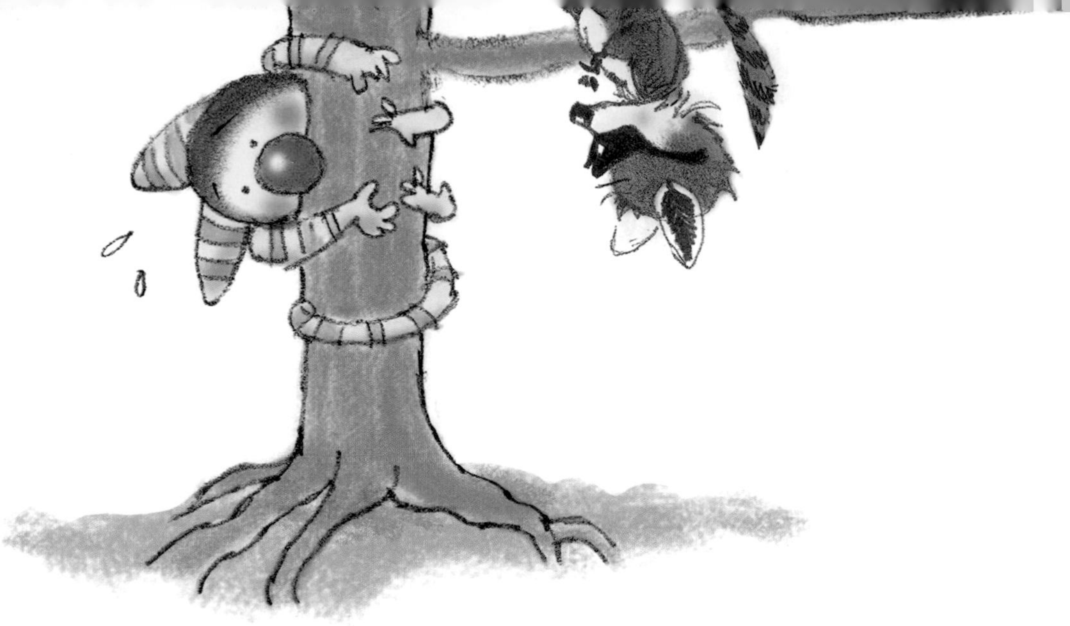

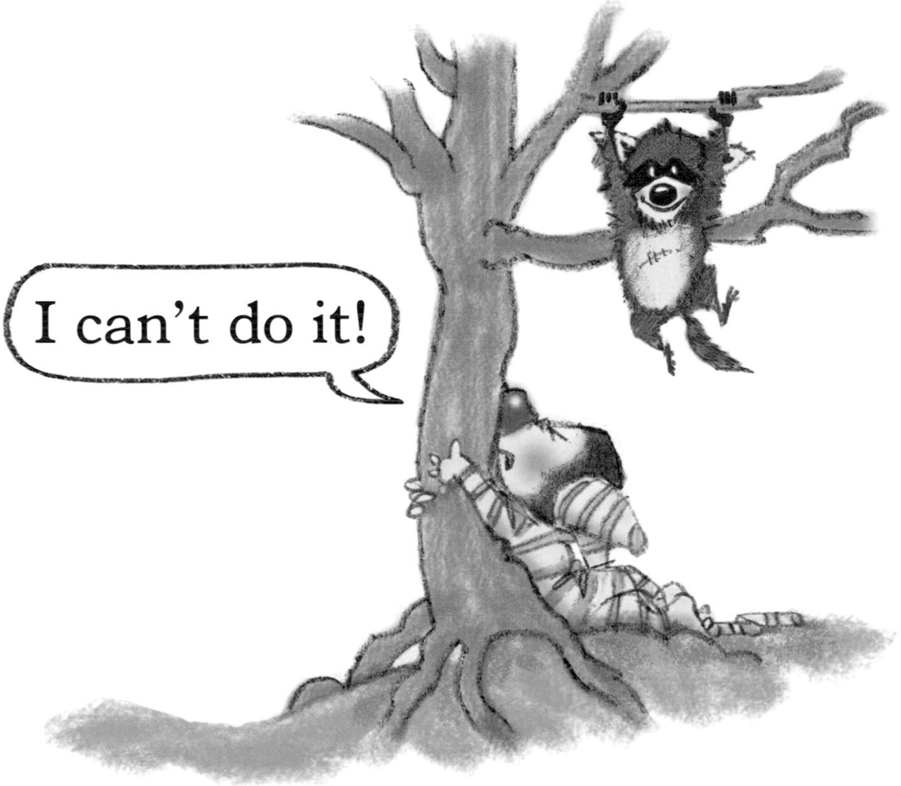
I can’t do it!

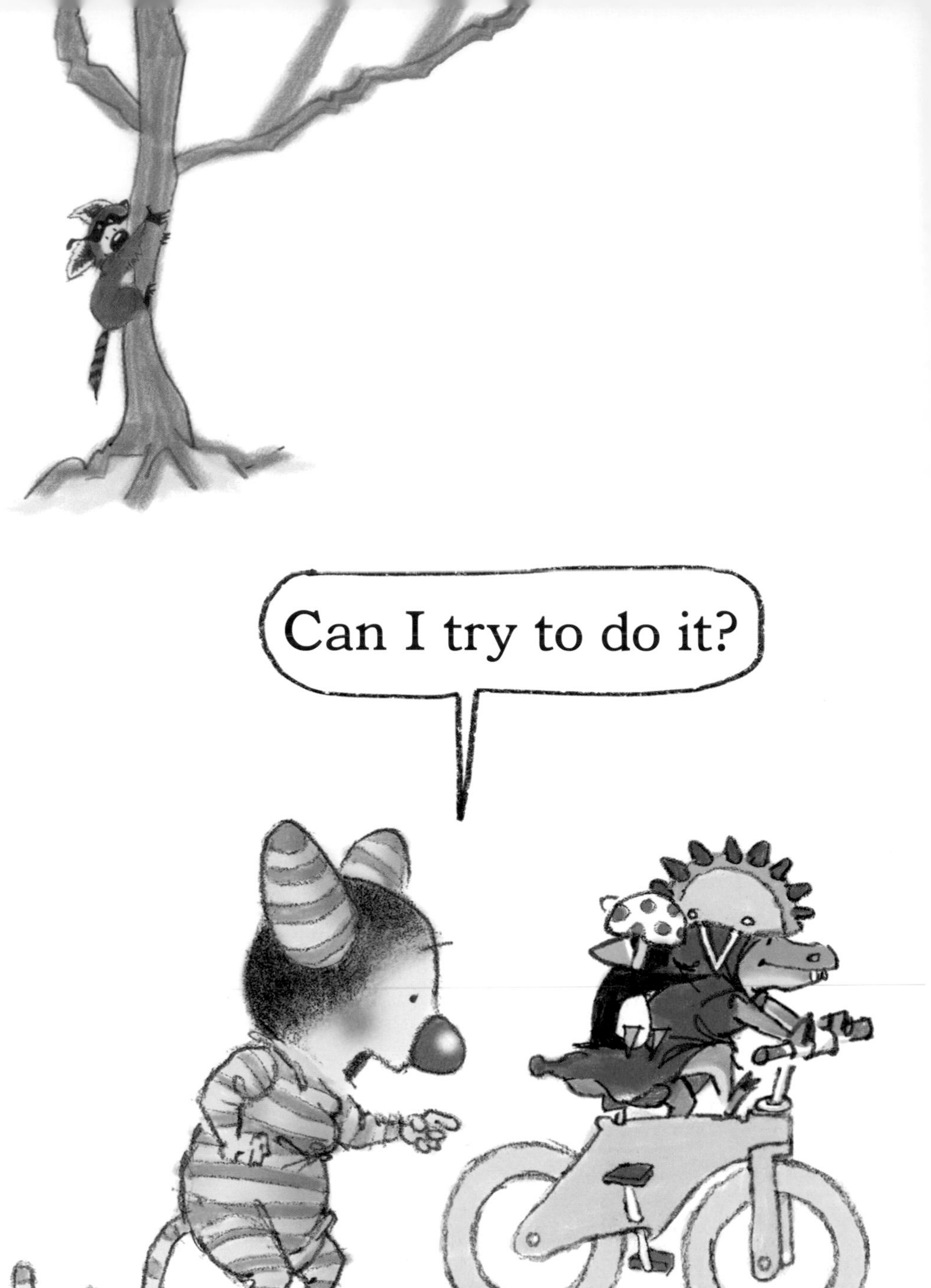
Can I try to do it?

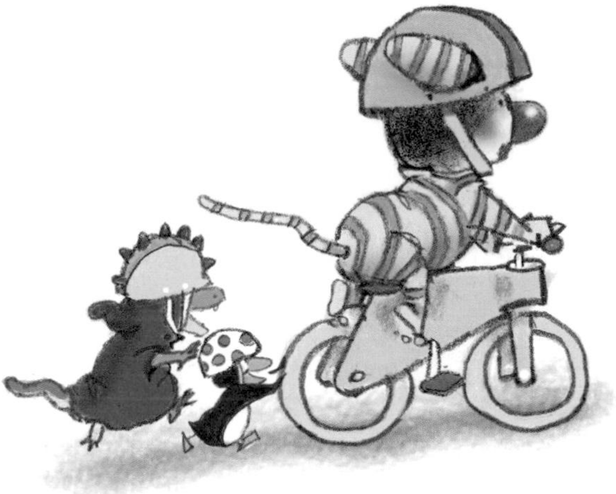

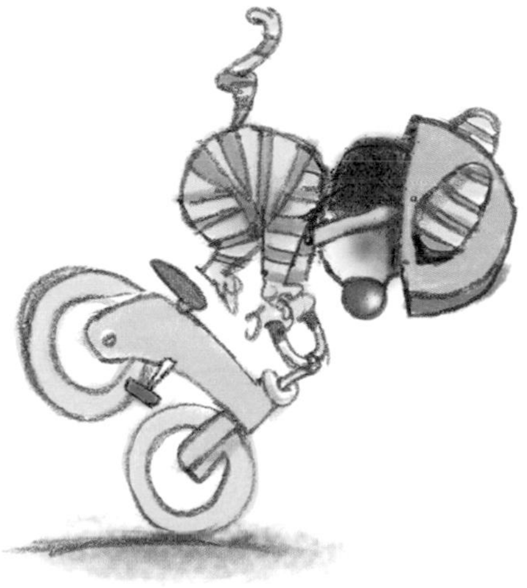

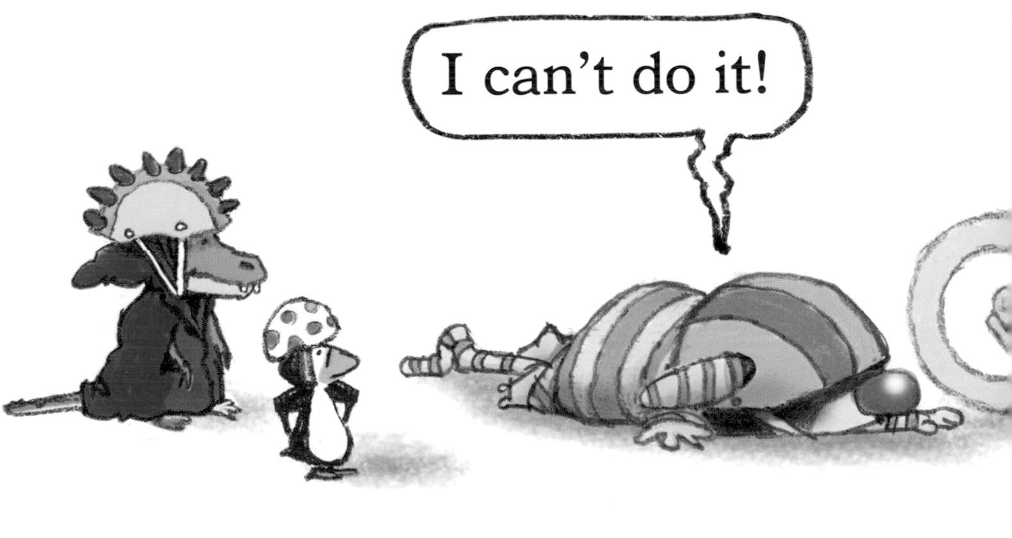
I can’t do it!

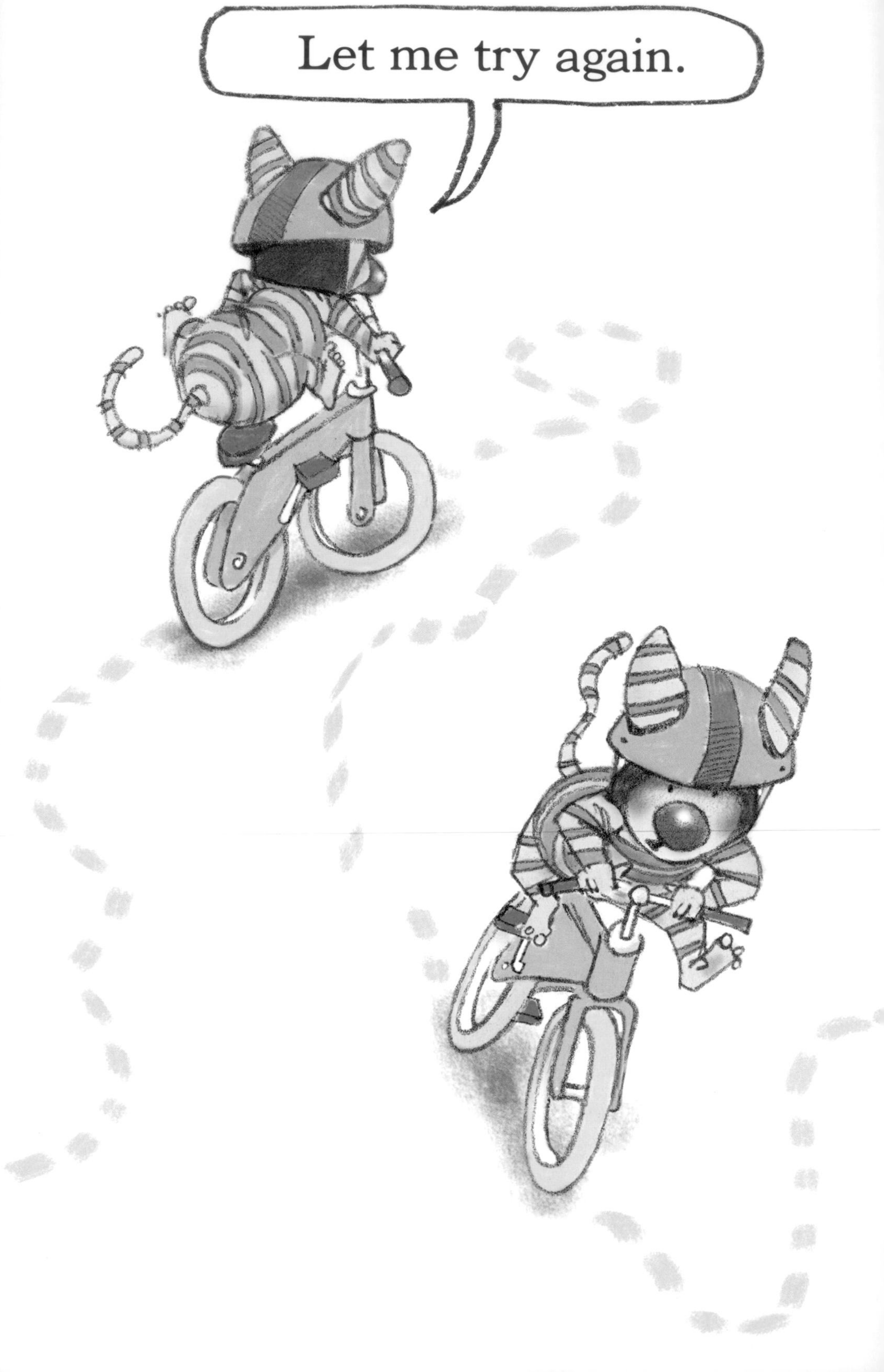
Let me try again.

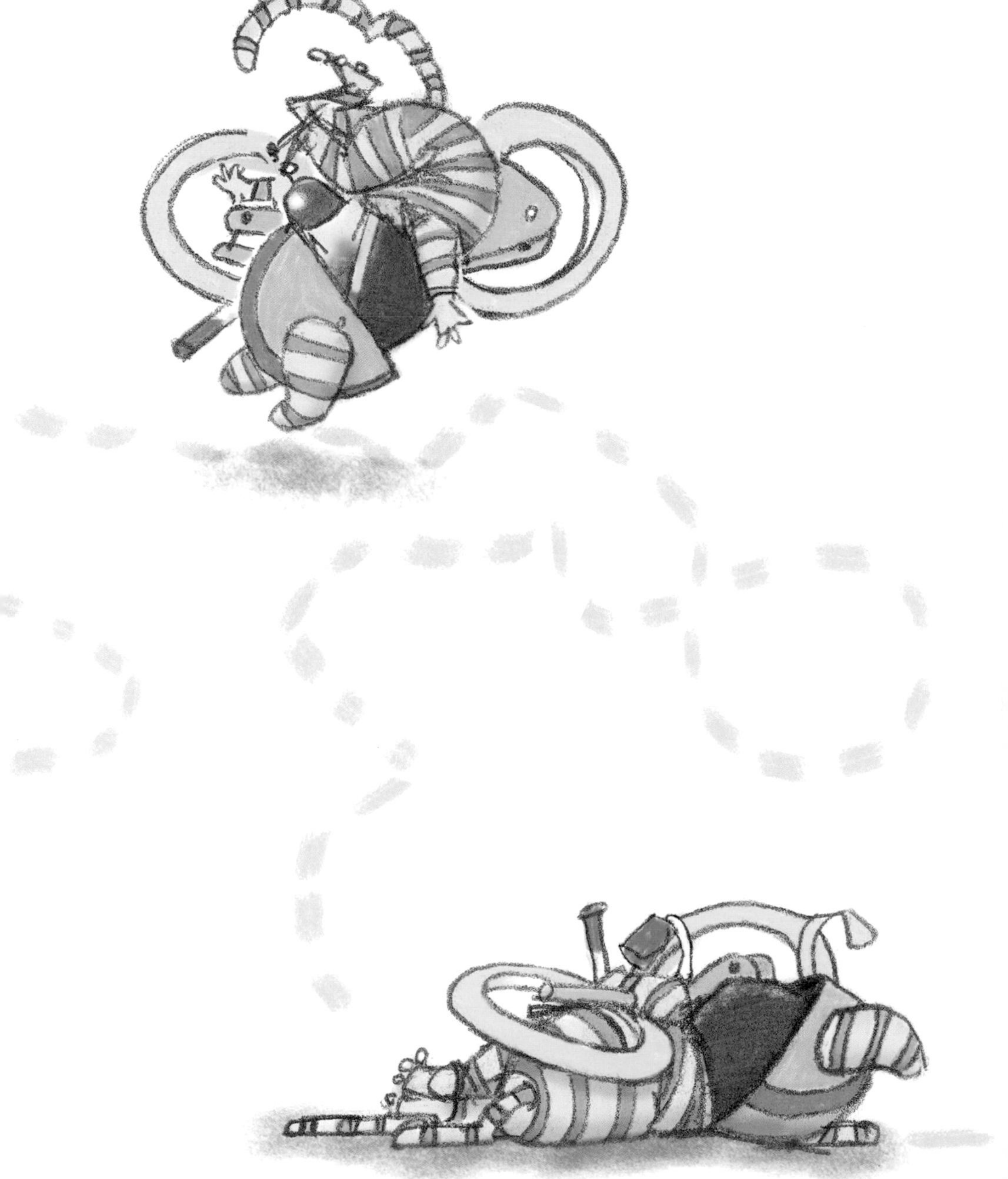

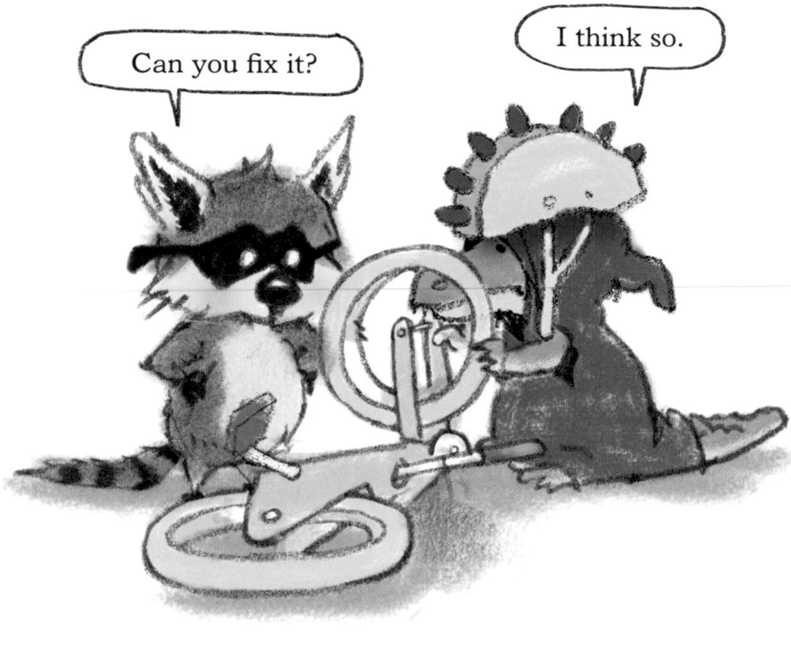
Can you fix it?
I think so.

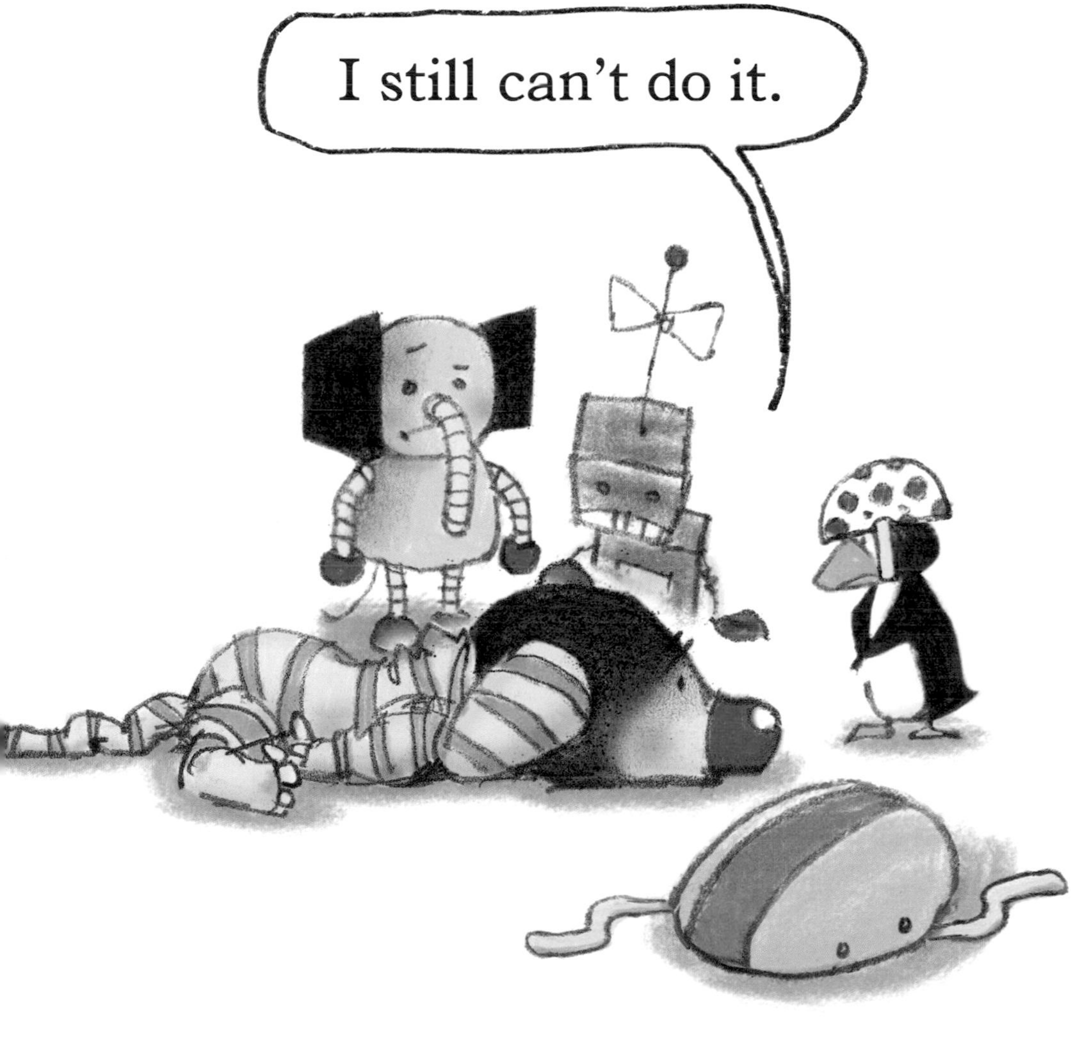
I still can't do it.

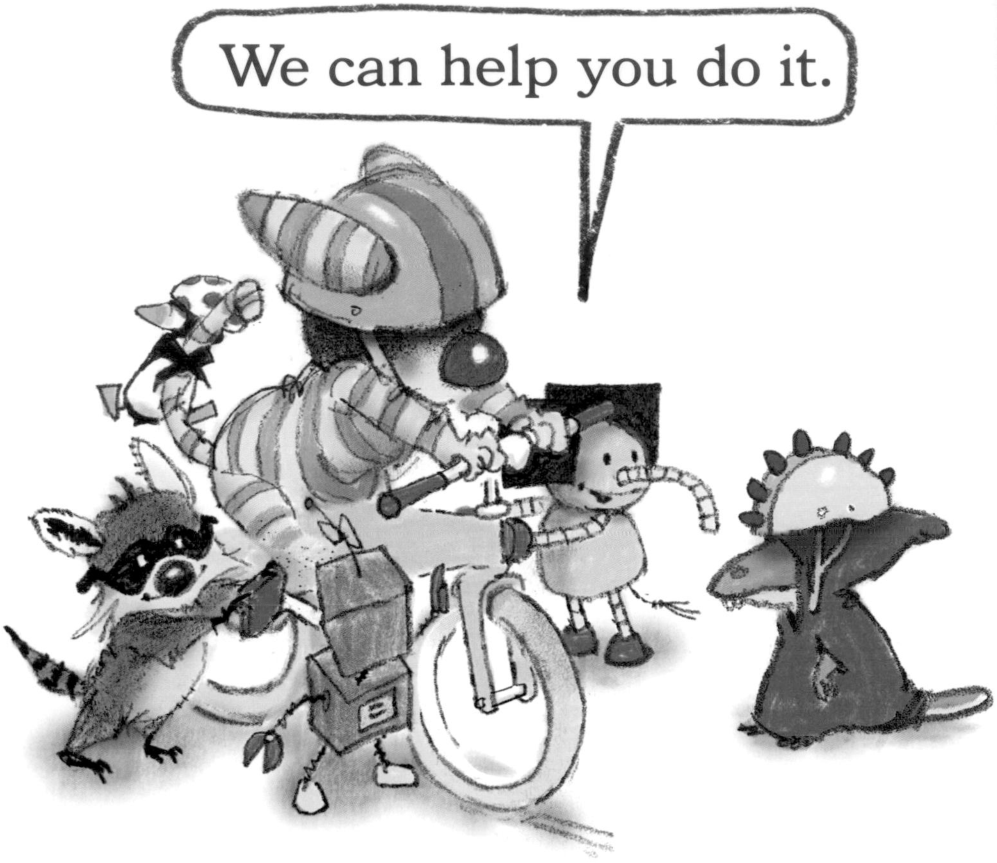
We can help you do it.

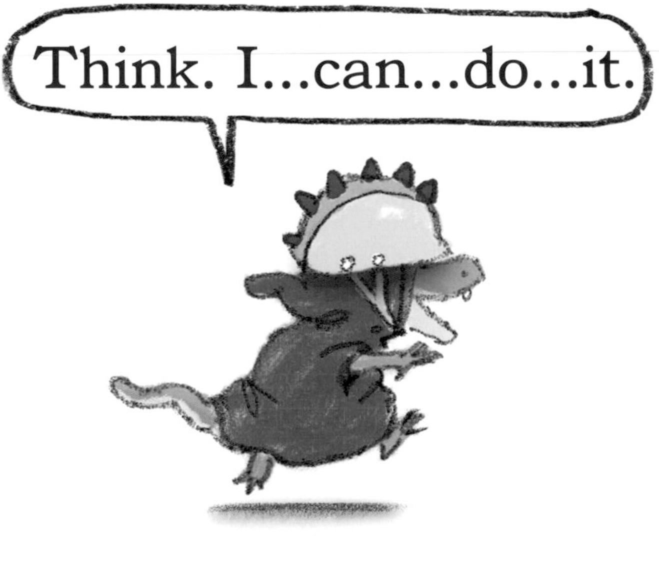
Think. I...can...do...it.

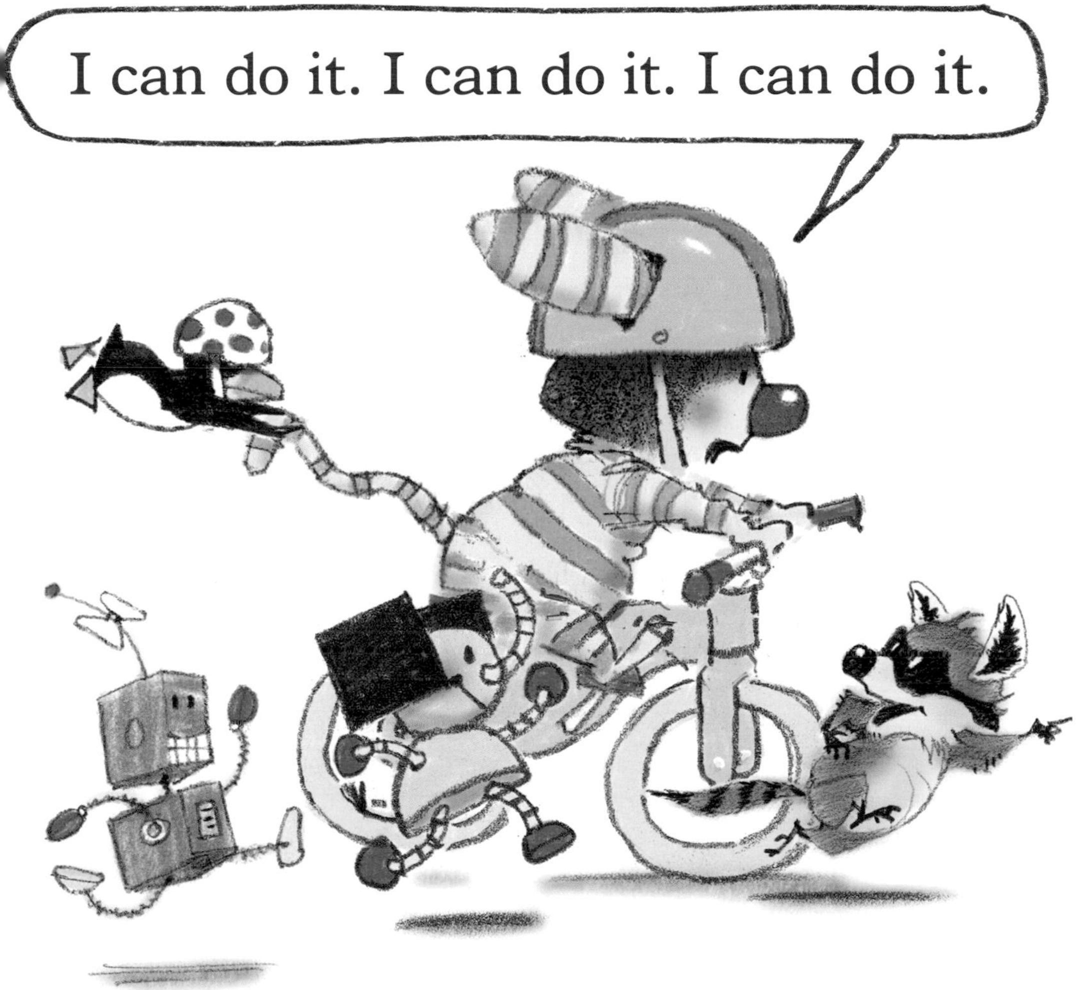
I can do it. I can do it. I can do it.

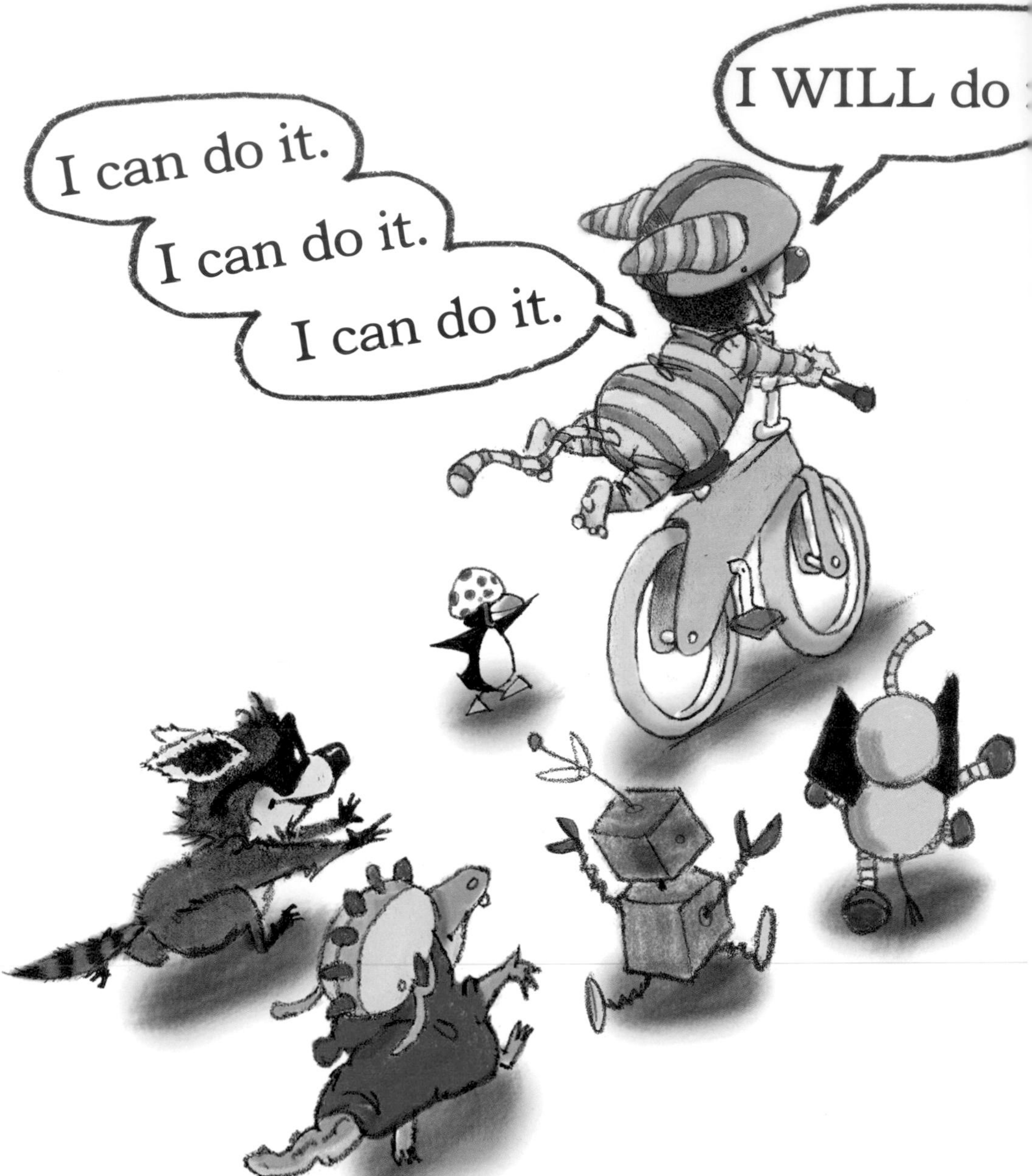
I can do it.
I can do it.
I can do it.
I WILL do

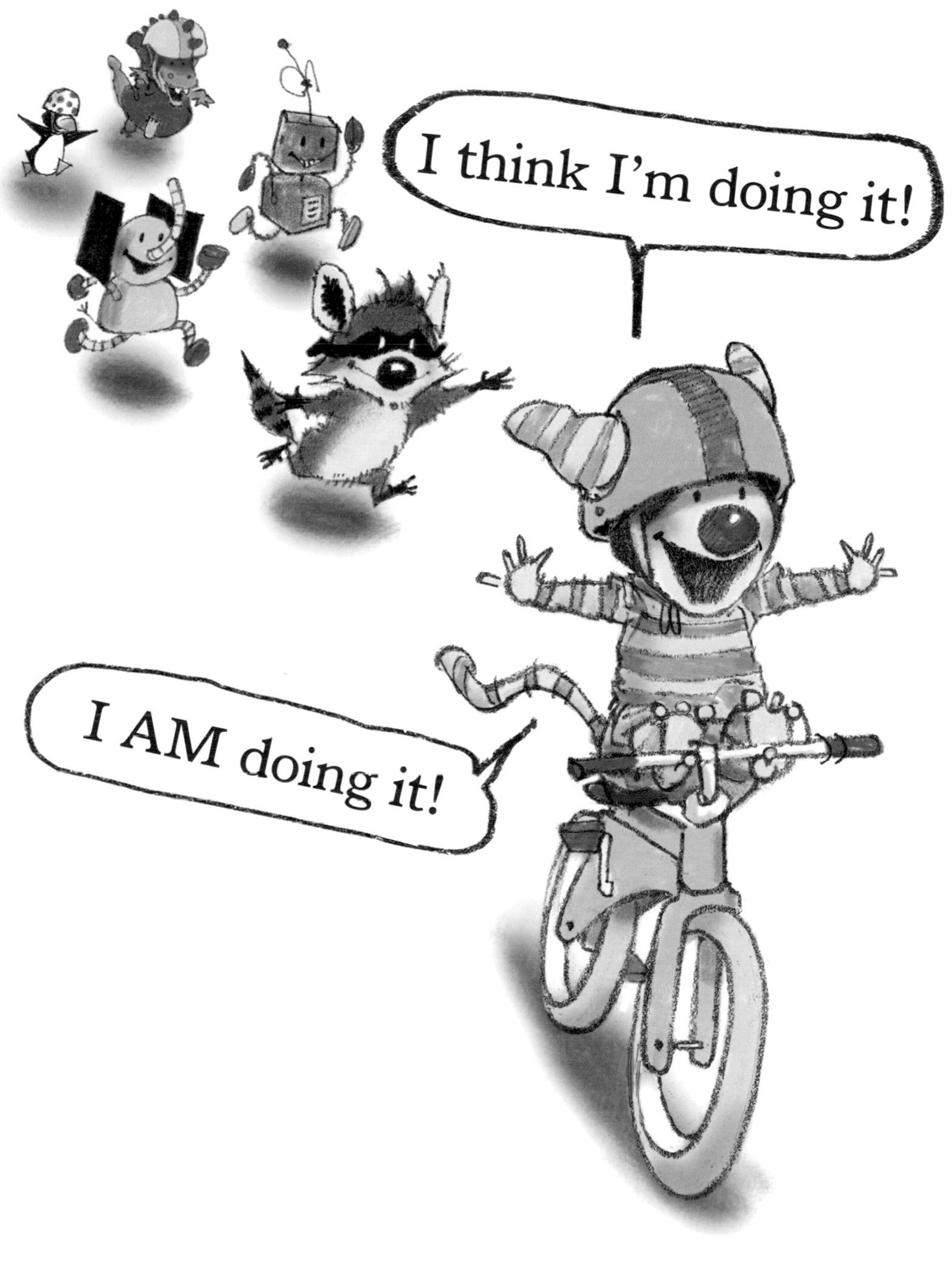
I think I'm doing it!
I AM doing it!

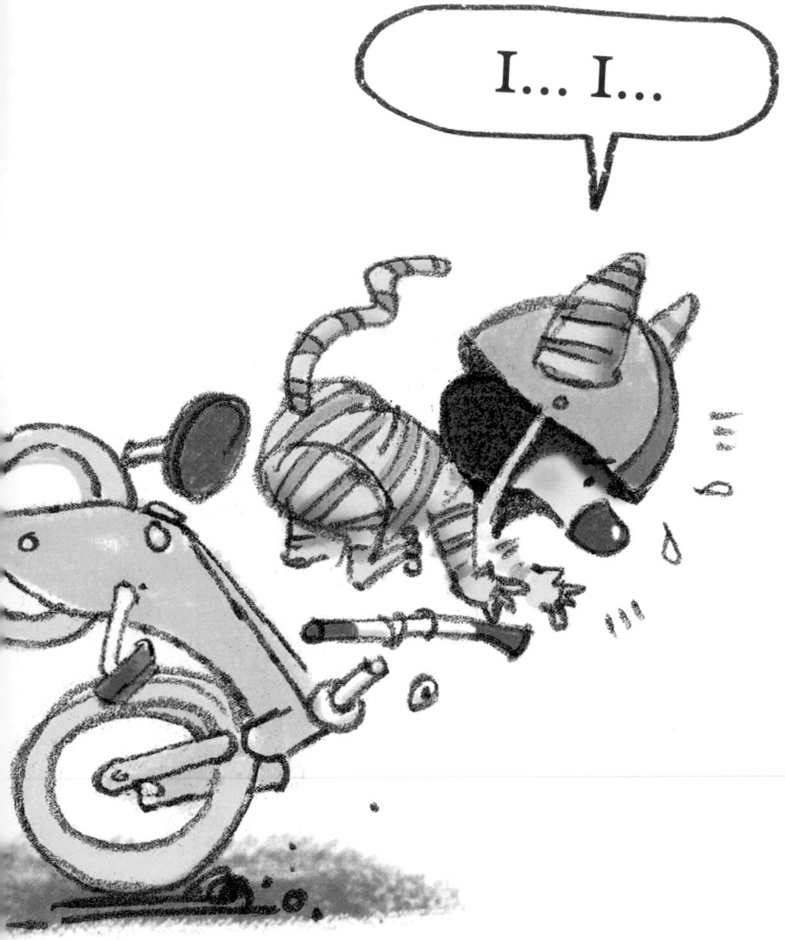
I… I…

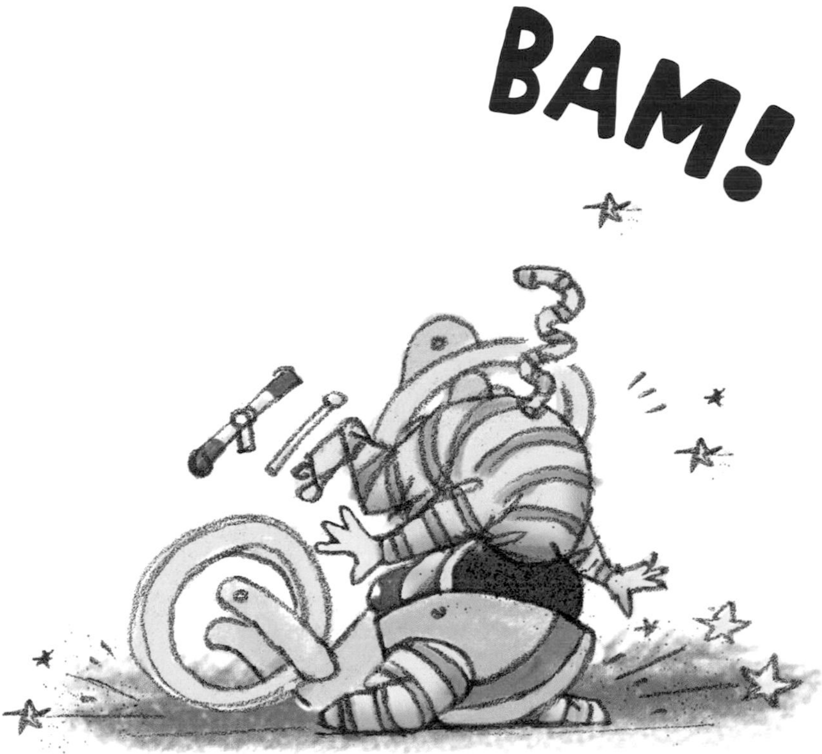
BAM!

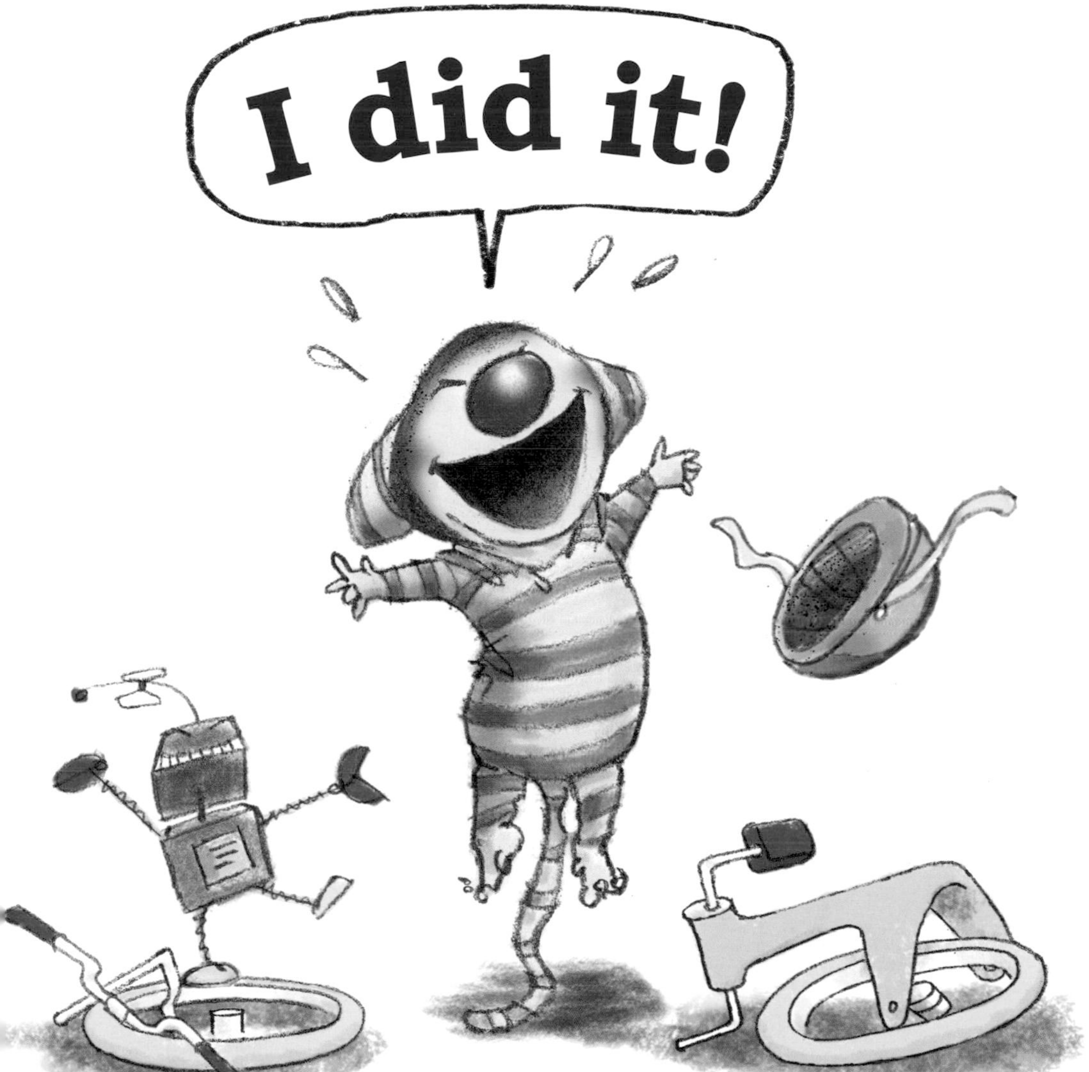
I did it!

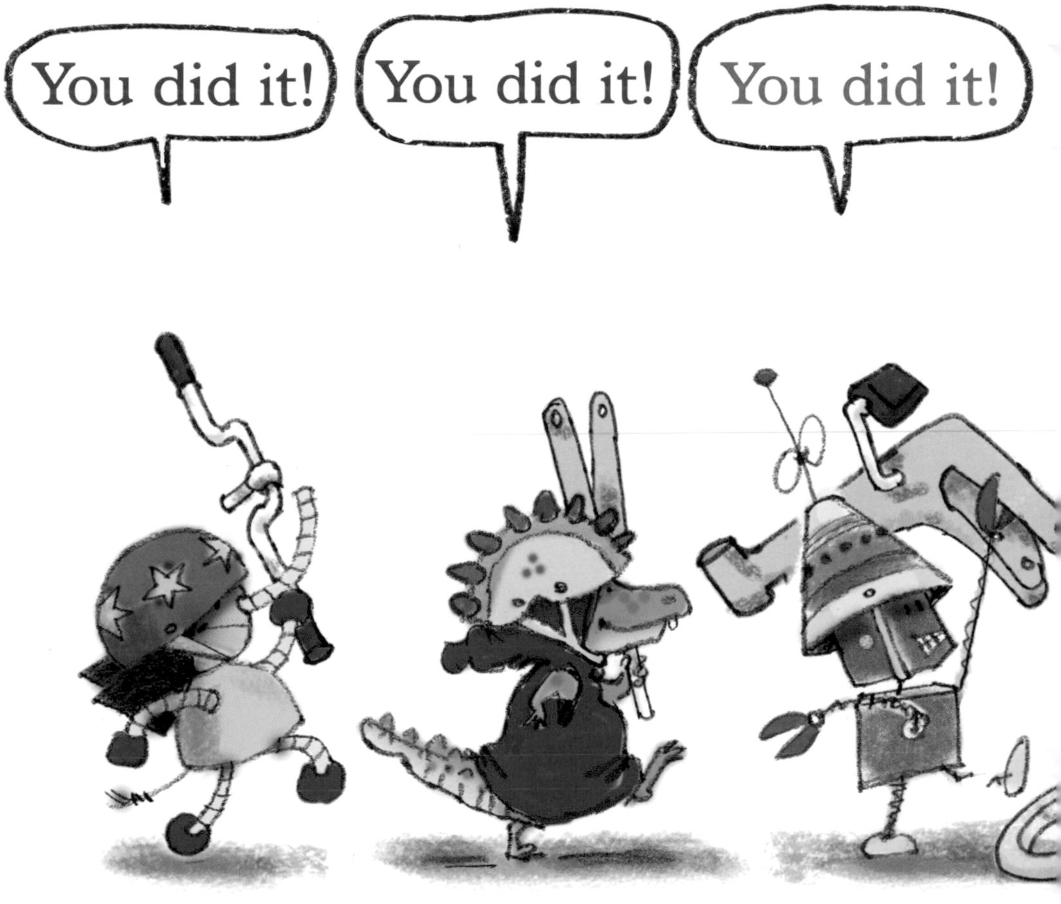
You did it!
You did it!
You did it!

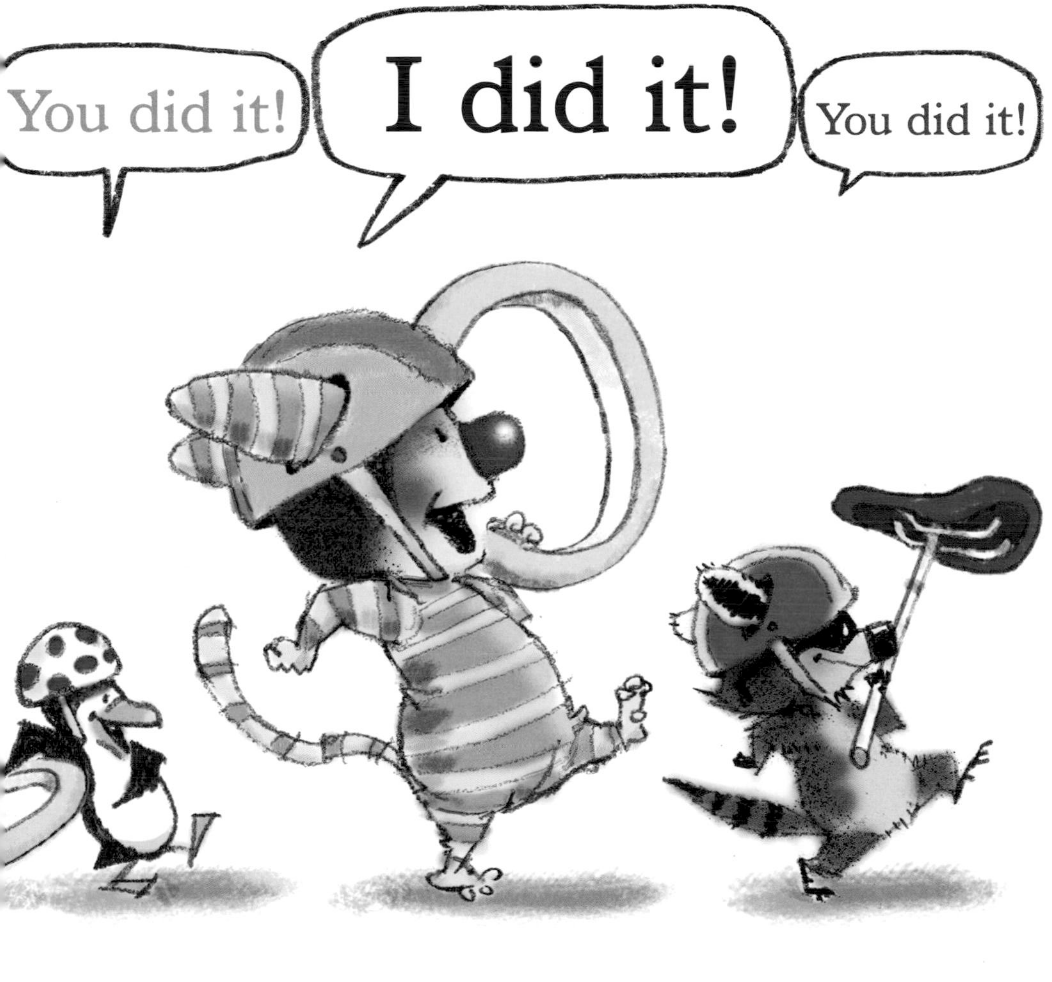
You did it!
I did it!
You did it!

For anyone who ever thought, "I can't do it."

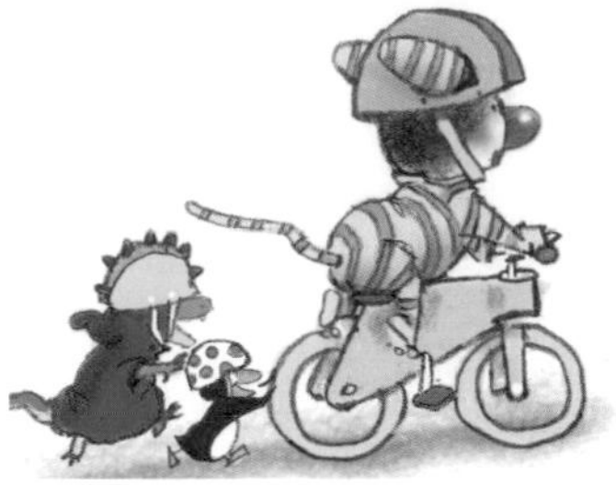

I Like to Read® Comics instill confidence and the joy of reading in new readers. Created by award-winning artists as well as talented newcomers,these imaginative books support beginners' reading comprehension with extensive visual support.

We want to hear every new reader say, "I like to read comics!"

Visit our website for flash cards, activities, and more about the series:
www.holidayhouse.com/ILiketoRead
#ILTR

Printed and bound in May 2022 at C&C Offset, Shenzhen, China.
The artwork was created with pencil lines and digital color.
www.holidayhouse.com

First Edition
1 3 5 7 9 10 8 6 4 2

Library of Congress Cataloging-in-Publication Data
Names: Emberley, Michael, author, illustrator.
Title: I did it! / Michael Emberley.
Other titles: I like to read comics.
Description: [First edition] | New York : Holiday House, [2022] | Series: I like to read comics | Audience: Ages 4-8 | Audience: Grades K-1
Summary: A girl tries and tries again to learn to ride a bicycle and all her friends provide words of encouragement.
Identifiers: LCCN 2021041641 | ISBN 9780823446513 (hardcover)
Subjects: LCSH: Cycling—Comic books, strips, etc. | Cycling—Juvenile fiction. | Friendship—Comic books, strips, etc. | Friendship—Juvenile fiction. | Graphic novels. | CYAC: Graphic novels. | Cycling—Fiction. Friendship—Fiction. | LCGFT: Graphic novels.
Classification: LCC PZ7.7.E456 Iad | DDC 741.5/973—dc23
LC record available at https://lccn.loc.gov/2021041641

ISBN: 978-0-8234-4651-3 (hardcover)